London Borough of Tower Hamlets

91000008171701

D1495139

CARRIE

and the Roller Boots

First published in 2023 in Great Britain by
Barrington Stoke Ltd
18 Walker Street, Edinburgh, EH3 7LP

www.barringtonstoke.co.uk

Text © 2023 Lisa Thompson
Illustrations © 2023 Jess Rose

A CIP catalogue record for this book is available
from the British Library upon request

ISBN: 978-1-80090-189-6

Printed by Hussar Books, Poland

This book is in a super-readable format for young readers
beginning their independent reading journey.

CARRIE
and the Roller Boots

LISA THOMPSON

Illustrated by
JESS ROSE

Barrington Stoke

For my roller-skating partner, Sylvia

Contents

Chapter 1

The TV Show

One Saturday, Sidney and his mum went to Carrie's house to have pizzas. Carrie was Sidney's best friend, and she was very happy he was coming over.

They were going to watch their favourite television talent show together – *Entertain Us!*

Carrie and Sidney sat on the sofa in front of the television. Carrie picked up a big bit of pizza.

"We can pretend that we are judges on *Entertain Us!*" said Sidney.

"Yes!" said Carrie. "Let's give the contestants a score out of ten."

The first contestant was a man
who sang a song and played the guitar.
Carrie thought he was a bit boring.
The man finished the song.

"Four out of ten!" said Carrie.

"Five out of ten!" said Sidney.

They both giggled.

The next person was a woman
who told some jokes, and then came a
tightrope walker.

Carrie and Sidney gave their scores
again.

"This show is a bit like Friday Fun Time at school, isn't it?" said Carrie.

Sidney had too much pizza in his mouth to say anything. He nodded.

Once a month in Friday Assembly, the pupils got a chance to show their special talent, like reading a poem or doing a magic trick or playing the recorder.

"I'm going to take part in the next Friday Fun Time," said Sidney. "I'm going to tap-dance! I've been practising every day."

Carrie grinned. "You'll be brilliant, Sidney!" she said.

"What's your special talent, Carrie?" asked Sidney.

Carrie thought about it for a moment.

"I don't know," said Carrie. "I don't think I'm good at anything."

"Everyone is good at something," said Sidney. "You just need to find what it is."

Chapter 2

The Roller-Skating Girl

As Carrie and Sidney watched the talent show, Carrie thought about what her special talent might be. If she knew what it was, then maybe she could take part in Friday Fun Time too?

Carrie was just picking up another bit of pizza when the next contestant whooshed onto the stage on the television.

"She's wearing roller boots!" said Carrie.

The girl was also wearing a silver jumpsuit that sparkled under the stage lights.

"She looks amazing!" said Sidney.

The music began, and the girl on roller boots began to dance.

Carrie watched as the girl jumped and twisted into the air. She was incredible! Next, the girl crouched down low and then sprang up high and did so many spins that Carrie felt dizzy.

When the music came to an end, the girl did a cartwheel, then dropped onto her knees with her arms high above her head.

Carrie dropped her pizza slice onto her plate and began to clap.

"Ten out of ten!" said Carrie.

Sidney grinned and clapped too. "Ten out of ten from me as well!" said Sidney.

Carrie then had a brilliant idea. Skating was going to be her special talent! If she had some roller boots, then she could take part in Friday Fun Time too!

Chapter 3

The Charity Shop

On Monday, Sidney's mum worked late, so Sidney went home with Carrie and her dad after school. As they walked along, Sidney spotted something and stopped.

"Look, Carrie!" said Sidney.

He pointed to the window of a charity shop. Sitting on a shelf in the window was a pair of bright yellow roller boots.

They both rushed to the shop window to see better. The roller boots had blue laces and red wheels, and beside them were some knee and elbow pads.

"Skating is my special talent, and those are just what I need!" said Carrie.

Carrie's dad came over to look at the boots too.

"Shall we go inside and see how much they are?" said Carrie's dad.

Carrie's tummy fizzed with excitement. Her dad might buy the roller boots for her!

The man in the shop got the roller boots from the window, and Carrie's dad checked the size and the price.

"It looks like you're in luck, Carrie," he said. "They're your size and they're cheap. Would you like them?"

Carrie nodded. "Oh yes, please!" she said. She gave her dad a big hug.

As they walked home, Carrie turned to Sidney.

"We can both take part in Friday Fun Time now!" said Carrie. "We can do a routine together. You can tap-dance and I can skate!"

Sidney didn't answer right away.

Then he said, "I don't think skating is going to be very easy, Carrie. It might take a lot of practice."

But Carrie wasn't listening.

She was thinking about all the twirls, spins and jumps she'd do in her new roller boots.

Chapter 4

A First Try

When they got back to Carrie's house, Carrie quickly changed out of her school uniform and put on her cycling helmet and the new elbow and knee pads. Carrie sat on a garden chair on their patio, and her dad helped her to put the boots on.

"Just take it steady," said Carrie's dad. "I'll be inside if you need me."

Carrie stood up, but she was very wobbly. The boots were heavy and felt weird.

Carrie thought about the girl in the silver jumpsuit on the TV who had twirled around the stage and jumped into the air. It couldn't be that hard, could it?

She held her arms out and lifted
up her foot. But when she put her foot
down again, the boot began to roll away.

"Be careful!" said Sidney.

Carrie tried to glide her other foot along the ground, just like the girl in the silver jumpsuit, but the boots rolled in different directions and she fell backwards onto her bottom.

"Ouch!" she said.

Sidney rushed over and helped her up.

"Maybe I should hold your hand, Carrie?" said Sidney.

But Carrie didn't want Sidney to help. She wanted to be brilliant straight away.

"No, thank you," said Carrie.

She tried again, but this time she fell forwards onto the knee pads.

"I don't understand it," said Carrie. "Skating is going to be my special talent! Why am I not very good at it?"

Sidney helped Carrie to stand up again.

"You can't be good on your first try, Carrie," said Sidney. "At my first tap-dancing lesson, I couldn't even do a shuffle ball change!"

Carrie didn't know what Sidney was talking about, but she was too busy standing up and not falling over to ask.

After Carrie fell over for the third time, she tried not to cry.

"You will get better if you keep trying," said Sidney. "My tap-dancing teacher says that the more you practise the more you shine!"

But Carrie thought that practising sounded boring. She wanted to be a brilliant skater right now!

Chapter 5

The Dance Routine

The next day in school, Carrie and Sidney met up in the playground at break-time.

"I've been thinking, Carrie," said Sidney. "Why don't you take part in next month's Friday Fun Time instead? Then you'll have more time to practise."

But Carrie didn't want to wait for a whole month.

"No. I want to do a routine with you next week," said Carrie. "I know. Let's practise now! I'll pretend that I've got my roller boots on, and you can pretend that you've got your tap shoes."

Sidney shrugged. "OK," he said. "But it won't be as easy when you've got real roller boots on."

Carrie didn't listen to Sidney. "Let's start with you tap-dancing in the middle, and I'll skate in a circle around you," she said.

"Then I can do a jump and a cartwheel, and we'll finish with us both spinning," she went on.

"I think it sounds a bit hard, Carrie," said Sidney slowly. "You did fall over a lot when you tried your roller boots out, remember?"

Carrie frowned.

"But we've got ages until Friday Fun Time, so I'll be really good by then!" said Carrie.

"I don't know, Carrie," said Sidney. "I've been practising tap-dancing for weeks and weeks, and it's still very hard."

But Carrie was too busy spinning around and thinking about all the other moves she'd do on her roller boots to listen.

*

They practised their dance every day in school, and each time, Sidney asked Carrie if she'd had a go at her skating at home too. But every day, Carrie had an excuse.

"I was going to, but I was playing with my rabbits," said Carrie. "They get bored if I don't play with them."

"Let's practise at your house at the weekend," said Sidney. "But this time with your roller boots and my tap shoes."

"Yes!" said Carrie. "We're going to be amazing!"

Chapter 6

Practice Time

On Saturday morning, Sidney went to Carrie's house so that they could try out their routine together.

Sidney put his tap shoes on as Carrie put her feet into the roller boots. She had forgotten how heavy and weird they felt. She was starting to worry about the jumps, spins and cartwheel she had planned to do in the dance.

Maybe Sidney was right? Maybe she should have been practising every day?

Carrie stood up and wobbled.

"I'll hold your hand," said Sidney. This time Carrie didn't say no.

She pushed her feet forwards, and after a few slip-ups, the roller boots began to feel less weird.

"That's it, Carrie!" said Sidney. "You're doing it!"

Carrie grinned. She was skating!

She even did a little spin, but that was more by accident than on purpose.

"I can skate!" said Carrie.

"Well done, Carrie!" said Sidney. "You're getting the hang of it now."

"I'll practise the jumps, spins and cartwheel tomorrow," said Carrie. "And then our dance routine will be perfect!"

Sidney wasn't so sure. "Maybe it's best to keep the dance simple and you just skate," said Sidney. "You don't need to do any jumps, spins or cartwheels."

But Carrie shook her head. She wanted to show everyone her amazing special talent!

Chapter 7

The Last Rehearsal

Carrie practised her skating every evening after school, but she was too scared to jump, spin or cartwheel in case she fell over.

In fact, it was hard to even stand up without Sidney there holding her hand.

She felt bad – the dance routine had been all her idea, and she still couldn't do it properly! She was letting Sidney down.

On the day before Friday Fun Time, Sidney went back to Carrie's house after school for one last practice.

Carrie hadn't said much that day in school. What was wrong? He finished tying his tap shoes while she put her roller boots on.

"Are you OK, Carrie?" said Sidney.

Carrie shrugged and looked sad. "I've been thinking about Friday Fun Time," said Carrie. "I think it might be a good idea if you did the dance on your own."

"Why, Carrie?" said Sidney. "We've practised every break-time, and you've been practising after school, haven't you?"

Carrie nodded. "Yes, but I still can't do all the moves," said Carrie. "In fact, I can't do any of them! So maybe you'll be better off without me."

Sidney didn't say anything, and Carrie thought he might be angry with her, but then he suddenly grinned.

"Of course we can still do the routine together!" said Sidney.

"Really?" said Carrie. "But you were right – I don't have time to practise the jump, the spin or the cartwheel."

"You don't need to do any of those things to make it look special," said Sidney. "I've got an idea! Let's practise again. And this time keep holding on to my hand."

Chapter 8

Friday Fun Time

When they got to school the next day, Carrie saw Sidney standing with his mum with his shiny black tap shoes under his arm.

Carrie was holding her roller boots, and her tummy did a flip-flop. She and Sidney had practised their new routine, but she was still very, very nervous.

"Are you OK, Carrie?" said Carrie's dad.

Carrie shook her head. "I'm scared," she said.

"It's normal to feel nervous," said Carrie's dad. "But I've seen you and Sidney practising, and I know you are going to be brilliant."

Sidney looked over at her and gave a thumbs-up, which made her feel a bit better.

They went to class to do the register, and then all of the children walked into the hall.

Carrie and Sidney sat with another boy and girl who were taking part in Friday Fun Time as well.

Carrie put her roller boots on, and Sidney tied his tap shoes so that they were ready when it was their turn.

The boy went first. His special talent was juggling, and he was very good and only dropped two balls in his whole routine.

When it was the girl's turn, she went over to a drum kit that was set up in the corner of the hall. She could drum really quickly, and the beats made Carrie's heart thump even harder.

Next, it was Carrie and Sidney's turn. They stood up. Carrie was really scared, and her knees were shaking.

"At least there are no judges scoring us out of ten like on *Entertain Us!*" whispered Sidney. "Just do everything like we practised. OK?"

Carrie nodded. She held Sidney's hand as she skated to the front of the hall. Sidney's feet tip-tapped beside her.

Their dance began. Sidney took Carrie's hand, and they were off. Carrie rolled along on her roller boots as Sidney tap-danced beside her.

Carrie wiggled her hips as she went along, and Sidney ducked under her arm and did a twirl, tap-dancing at the same time.

There was a moment when Carrie really wobbled and thought she was going to fall, but she held on tight to Sidney's hand.

They came to the last part of the dance, and Carrie and Sidney held both of their hands together and whizzed around and around in a circle.

They came to a stop, and each held one hand up high in the air to finish. They had big grins on their faces. The audience burst out clapping.

Carrie was thrilled! Even though she'd had to hold Sidney's hand the whole time, she had skated! And their dance had been brilliant!

They went back to the side of the hall and sat down.

"You were fantastic, Carrie!" said Sidney. "Are you pleased you found your special talent?"

Carrie looked over at the girl who had been playing the drums, and then she turned to Sidney and grinned.

"I'm not sure if skating is my special talent after all," said Carrie. "I think I want to play the drums instead!"

Sidney gave a big sigh, and then they both laughed.